MENU 菜單

1000
THINGS TO
EAT
兒童英漢詞彙大書
食物1000詞

Researched and
edited by
Hannah Wood

Illustrated by Nikki Dyson

Additional editing by
Felicity Brooks and
Caroline Young

Designed by
Francesca Allen,
Claire Ever and
Kirsty Tizzard

商務印書館

Breakfast 早餐

Toast
吐司

Eggy bread
蛋香麵包

Bagel
百吉圈

Toasted muffin
烤鬆餅

Crumpet
小圓烤餅

Scotch pancakes
蘇格蘭煎餅

Brioche
法國奶油麵包

Croissant
牛角包

Pain au chocolat
朱古力酥

Strawberry jam
草莓果醬

Apricot jam
杏桃果醬

Cherry jam
櫻桃果醬

Raspberry jam
紅桑子果醬

Blackberry jam
黑莓果醬

Marmalade
柳橙醬

Lemon curd
檸檬酪

Honey
蜜糖

Peanut butter
花生醬

Maple syrup
楓糖漿

Golden syrup
金黃糖漿

Muesli
雜錦燕麥片

Granola
格蘭諾拉燕麥片

Porridge
燕麥粥

Cornflakes
玉米片

Fruit yogurt
水果乳酪

Eggs Benedict
班尼迪克蛋

Poached eggs
水波蛋

Eggs Florentine
菠菜口味班尼迪克蛋

Boiled egg and soldiers
水煮蛋配吐司條

Scrambled eggs
炒蛋

Sausages
香腸

Bacon
煙肉

Black pudding
血腸

Baked beans
焗豆

Fried bread
油炸麵包

Butter
牛油

Margarine
人造牛油

Tea
茶

Grapefruit juice
西柚汁

Apple juice
蘋果汁

Orange juice
橙汁

Milk
牛奶

Home-cooked food 家常菜

Vegetable soup
蔬菜湯

Mushroom soup
蘑菇湯

Minestrone soup
意式雜菜湯

Cauliflower cheese
焗芝士椰菜花

Spaghetti bolognese
波隆那肉醬意粉

Spaghetti and meatballs
肉丸意粉

Shepherd's pie
牧羊人餡餅

Chilli con carne
燉辣肉醬

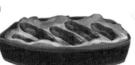
Toad in the hole
烤香腸布甸

Ratatouille
普羅旺斯燉菜

Roast beef and Yorkshire puddings
烤牛肉配約克郡布甸

Sausages and mash
香腸配薯蓉

Chicken Kiev
基輔炸雞

Chicken casserole
砂鍋雞

Gammon joint
醃豬腿

Roast pork shoulder
烤豬肩肉

Pork chops
豬排

Nut loaf
果仁糕

Beef Wellington
威靈頓牛排

Meatloaf
肉卷

Fish pie
魚餡餅

Macaroni cheese
芝士焗通心粉

Roast leg of lamb
烤羊腿

Beef stew
燉牛肉

Fried egg
煎蛋

Roast chicken
烤雞

Ways of cooking 烹飪方法

Barbecued pork ribs
烤豬肋骨

Stewed lamb
燉羊肉

Roast potatoes
烤馬鈴薯

Sautéed potatoes
煎馬鈴薯

French fries
薯條

Baked potato
焗薯

Boiled potatoes
水煮馬鈴薯

Mashed potato
馬鈴薯蓉

Grilled salmon
炙烤三文魚

Stir-fried vegetables
炒雜菜

Steamed broccoli
蒸西蘭花

Cheese fondue
芝士火鍋

Tomato soup
番茄湯

Home baking
居家烘焙

Shortbread
奶油酥餅

Gingerbread people
薑餅人

Chocolate-chip cookies
朱古力碎曲奇

Scones
英國鬆餅

Brownies
布朗尼

Rice crispy cakes
脆米蛋糕

Tiffin
蒂芬蛋糕

Rocky road
石板街

Apple pie
蘋果餡餅

Apple crumble
蘋果金寶

Lemon tart
檸檬撻

Banoffee pie
香蕉太妃餡餅

Apple strudel
維也納蘋果卷

Streuselkuchen
奶酥蛋糕

Cheesecake
芝士蛋糕

Chelsea bun
切爾西麵包卷

Iced finger bun
糖霜手指條

Swiss roll
瑞士卷

Flapjack
燕麥酥

Fairy cakes
小仙子蛋糕

Jam tarts
果醬撻

Cupcake
杯子蛋糕

Victoria sponge
維多利亞海綿蛋糕

Carrot cake
甘筍蛋糕

Malt loaf
麥芽糖麵包

Meringue
蛋白酥

Madeira cake
馬德拉蛋糕

Coffee and walnut cake
咖啡核桃蛋糕

Battenberg cake
巴騰堡棋格蛋糕

Sticky toffee pudding
椰棗拖肥糖布甸

Chocolate teacake
朱古力蛋白霜茶點

Sable biscuits
薩布萊餅乾

Coconut macaroons
椰子球甜餅

Amaretti
意大利杏仁餅

Garibaldi biscuits
加里波底餅乾

The biscuit tin
餅乾罐

Anzac biscuits
澳新軍團餅乾

Afghan biscuit
阿富汗餅乾

Petit Beurré
不的波餅乾

Custard cream
吉士醬夾心餅

Pink wafers
粉紅威化餅

Bourbons
波旁餅

Florentines
佛羅倫斯脆餅

Ginger snap
薑餅乾

Marie biscuit
馬利餅

Rosette cookie
玫瑰花餅

Chocolate digestive
朱古力消化餅

Brandy snaps
白蘭地脆捲

Biscotti
意式脆餅

Carob
角豆

Mace
肉豆蔻乾皮

Spice cupboard
香料櫃

Cloves
丁香

Ginger
薑

Paprika
紅椒粉

Cardamom pods
小豆蔻

Cayenne pepper
卡宴辣椒

Chilli powder
辣椒粉

Mustard seeds
芥末籽

Juniper berries
杜松子

Cumin seeds
孜然

Nutmeg
肉豆蔻

Star anise
八角

Cinnamon sticks
肉桂條

Turmeric
薑黃

Fennel seeds
茴香籽

Saffron
番紅花

Garam masala
馬薩拉香料

Vanilla pods
香草莢

Coriander seeds
芫荽籽

Salt
鹽

Black pepper
黑胡椒

White pepper
白胡椒

Pink pepper
紅胡椒

Store cupboard 儲物櫃

White flour
白麵粉

Quinoa
藜麥

Polenta
粗玉米粉

Bulgur wheat
保加利亞小麥

Wholemeal flour
全麥麵粉

Buckwheat flour
蕎麥麵粉

Couscous
北非小米

Sesame seeds
芝麻

Poppy seeds
罌粟籽

Sunflower seeds
葵花籽

Pearl barley
洋薏米

Pumpkin seeds
南瓜籽

Pecans
碧根果仁

Brazil nuts
巴西堅果

Pine nuts
松子

Pistachios
開心果

Almonds
杏仁

White sugar
白糖

Muscovado sugar
黑糖

Peanuts
花生

Macadamia nuts
夏威夷果仁

Walnuts
核桃

Demerara sugar
德麥拉拉蔗糖

Brown sugar
紅糖

Chestnuts
栗子

Hazelnuts
榛子

Cashews
腰果

Icing sugar
糖粉

Quail eggs
鵪鶉蛋

Chicken egg
雞蛋

Duck egg
鴨蛋

Goose egg
鵝蛋

Ostrich egg
鴕鳥蛋

Raisins
葡萄乾

Currants
無核小葡萄乾

Sultanas
蘇丹娜青葡萄乾

Mixed peel
雜錦果皮

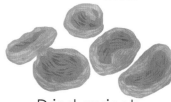
Dried apricots
杏脯乾

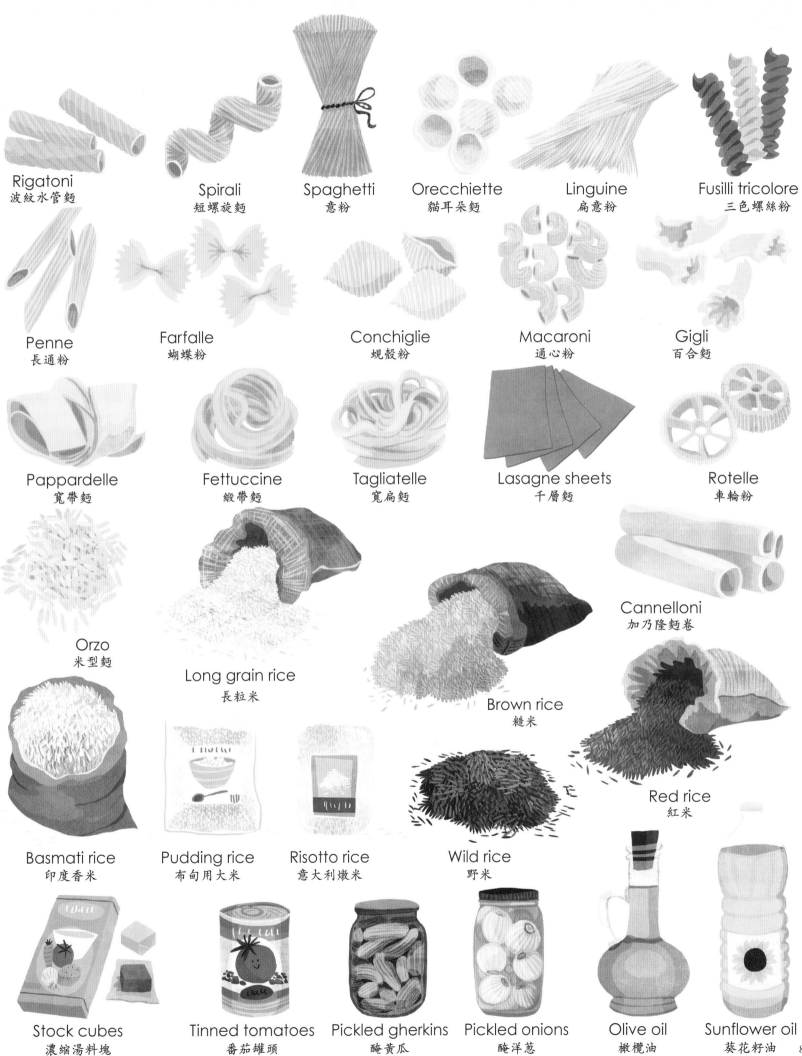

Rigatoni
波紋水管麵

Spirali
短螺旋麵

Spaghetti
意粉

Orecchiette
貓耳朵麵

Linguine
扁意粉

Fusilli tricolore
三色螺絲粉

Penne
長通粉

Farfalle
蝴蝶粉

Conchiglie
蜆殼粉

Macaroni
通心粉

Gigli
百合麵

Pappardelle
寬帶麵

Fettuccine
緞帶麵

Tagliatelle
寬扁麵

Lasagne sheets
千層麵

Rotelle
車輪粉

Orzo
米型麵

Long grain rice
長粒米

Brown rice
糙米

Cannelloni
加乃隆麵卷

Red rice
紅米

Basmati rice
印度香米

Pudding rice
布甸用大米

Risotto rice
意大利燉米

Wild rice
野米

Stock cubes
濃縮湯料塊

Tinned tomatoes
番茄罐頭

Pickled gherkins
醃黃瓜

Pickled onions
醃洋葱

Olive oil
橄欖油

Sunflower oil
葵花籽油

8

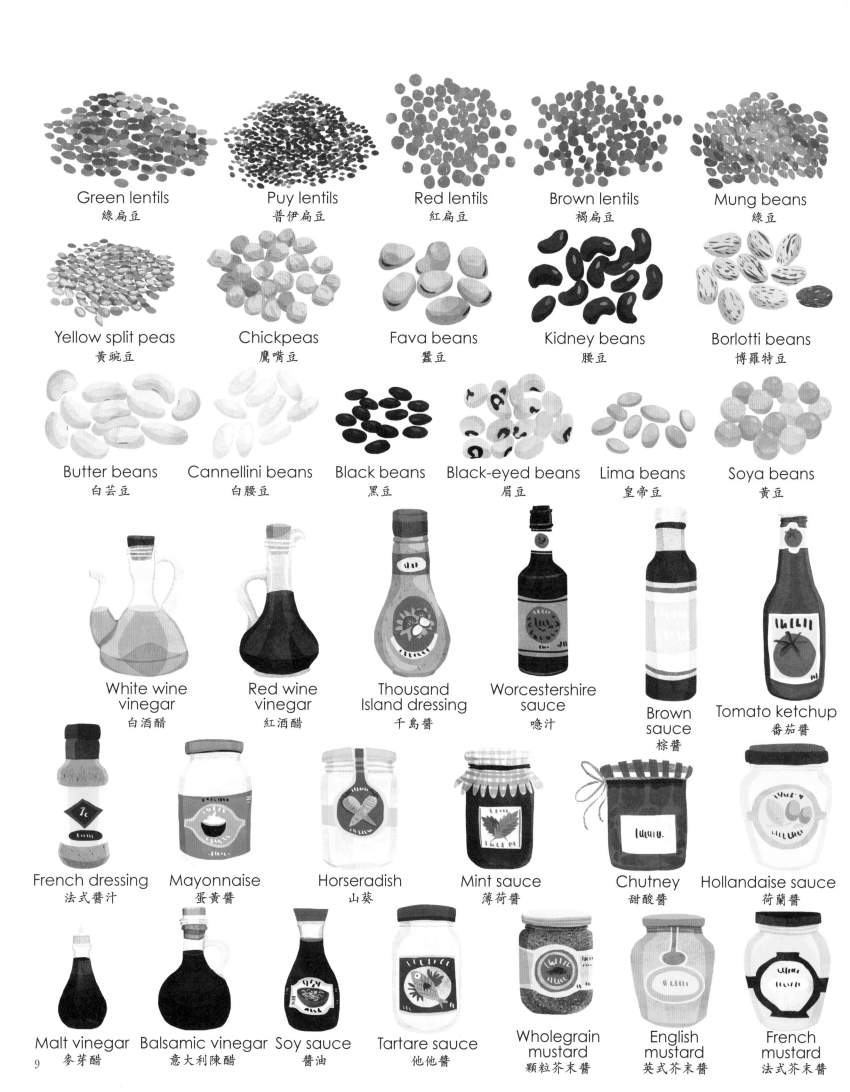

Green lentils
綠扁豆

Puy lentils
普伊扁豆

Red lentils
紅扁豆

Brown lentils
褐扁豆

Mung beans
綠豆

Yellow split peas
黃豌豆

Chickpeas
鷹嘴豆

Fava beans
蠶豆

Kidney beans
腰豆

Borlotti beans
博羅特豆

Butter beans
白芸豆

Cannellini beans
白腰豆

Black beans
黑豆

Black-eyed beans
眉豆

Lima beans
皇帝豆

Soya beans
黃豆

White wine vinegar
白酒醋

Red wine vinegar
紅酒醋

Thousand Island dressing
千島醬

Worcestershire sauce
喼汁

Brown sauce
棕醬

Tomato ketchup
番茄醬

French dressing
法式醬汁

Mayonnaise
蛋黃醬

Horseradish
山葵

Mint sauce
薄荷醬

Chutney
甜酸醬

Hollandaise sauce
荷蘭醬

Malt vinegar
麥芽醋

Balsamic vinegar
意大利陳醋

Soy sauce
醬油

Tartare sauce
他他醬

Wholegrain mustard
顆粒芥末醬

English mustard
英式芥末醬

French mustard
法式芥末醬

The bakery 麵包店

White bloomer
布魯姆麵包

Bread rolls
麵包卷

Tiger bread
老虎麵包

Sliced white bread
切片白麵包

Brown bread
黑麵包

Wholemeal bloomer
全麥布魯姆麵包

Plaited loaf
辮子麵包

Seeded loaf
谷物麵包

Cottage loaf
農夫包

Ciabatta
拖鞋麵包

Granary bread
全麥麵包

Cornbread
玉米麵包

Crispbread
薄脆餅乾

Pumpernickel
粗裸麥麵包

Baguette
法國長麵包

Rye bread
黑麥麵包

Focaccia
佛卡夏麵包

Challah
猶太哈拉麵包

Sourdough loaf
酵母麵包

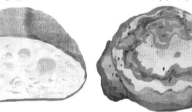
Cheese bread
芝士麵包

Chocolate éclair
朱古力閃電泡芙

Macaroons
馬卡龍

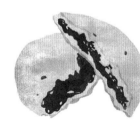
Eccles cake
葡萄乾餡餅

Madeleines
瑪德蓮貝殼蛋糕

Palmier
蝴蝶酥

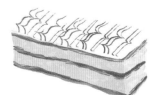
Millefeuille
千層酥

Egg tart
蛋撻

Fraisier cake
法式草莓蛋糕

Fruit tart
水果撻

Petits fours
花色小蛋糕

The greengrocer's 蔬菜水果店

Sweet orange	Satsuma	Kumquats	Clementine	Tangerine	Blood orange
甜橙	薩摩蜜柑	金橘	小柑橘	橘	血橙

Lemon	Pink grapefruit	Yellow grapefruit	Pomelo	Braeburn apple
檸檬	紅肉西柚	白肉西柚	柚子	布雷本蘋果

Cooking apple	Gala apple	Golden delicious apple	Granny Smith apple	Bosc pear	William pear
烹飪用蘋果	加拿蘋果	金冠蘋果	澳洲青蘋果	鴨梨	威廉梨

Bartlett pear	Conference pear	Nectarine	Peach	Quince	Medlar
巴梨	長啤梨	油桃	桃子	木梨	歐楂

Apricot	European plum	Japanese plum	Greengage	Black cherries	Morello cherries
杏子	西梅	李	青梅	黑櫻桃	酸櫻桃

Wild strawberries	Strawberries	Pineberry	Raspberries	Blackberries	Loquat
野草莓	草莓	菠蘿莓	紅桑子	黑莓	枇杷

| Blackcurrants 黑醋栗 | White currants 白醋栗 | Redcurrants 紅醋栗 | Black grapes 黑葡萄 | Red grapes 紅葡萄 | Green grapes 青葡萄 |

| Dewberries 露珠莓 | Boysenberries 波森莓 | Loganberries 楊莓 | Mulberries 桑椹 | Bilberries 山桑子 |

| Damsons 西洋李子 | Huckleberries 黑漿果 | Blueberries 藍莓 | Maqui berries 馬基莓 | Lingonberries 越橘 |

| Rhubarb 大黃 | Cranberries 蔓越莓 | Goji berries 杞子 | Goumi berries 木半夏 | Thimbleberries 糙莓 |

| Gooseberries 鵝莓 | Galia melon 加利亞甜瓜 | Watermelon 西瓜 | Honeydew melon 蜜瓜 |

| Prickly pear 仙人掌果 | Pomegranate 石榴 | Figs 無花果 | Persimmon 柿子 | Acerola 針葉櫻桃 |

Coconut
椰子

Plantains
大蕉

Bananas
香蕉

Cantaloupe
羅馬甜瓜

Pineapple
鳳梨

Dragon fruit
火龍果

Guava
番石榴

Mango
芒果

Sapodilla
人心果

Papaya
木瓜

Breadfruit
麵包果

Durian
榴槤

Jackfruit
大樹菠蘿

Soursop
刺果番荔枝

Custard apple
番荔枝

Açaí berries
巴西紫莓

Horned melon
刺角瓜

Star fruit
楊桃

Physalis
燈籠果

Ackee
西非荔枝果

Limes
青檸

Pepinos
人參果

Lychee
荔枝

Rambutan
紅毛丹

Mangosteen
山竹

Longan
龍眼

Limoncillo
西班牙青檸

Star apple
牛奶果

Naranjilla
奎東茄

Passion fruit
熱情果

Kiwi fruit
奇異果

Golden kiwi
金奇異果

Tamarind
羅望子

| Courgette 意大利青瓜 | Globe artichoke 洋薊 | Corn 玉米 | Samphire 海蘆筍 | Celery 芹菜 | Asparagus 蘆筍 |

| Aubergine 茄子 | Cauliflower 椰菜花 | Romanesco cauliflower 寶塔菜 | Red cabbage 紫椰菜 | Chicory 菊苣 | White cabbage 椰菜 |

| Caper berries 續隨子漿果 | Baby corn 珍珠筍 | Peppers 甜椒 | Bird's eye chillies 鳥眼辣椒 | Jalapeño chilli 墨西哥辣椒 | Scotch bonnet chilli 蘇格蘭帽辣椒 | Okra 秋葵 |

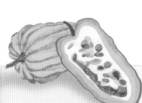     

| Bitter melon 苦瓜 | Beansprouts 豆芽 | Peas 豌豆 | Green beans 四季豆 | Sugar snap peas 甜豆 | Mangetout 荷蘭豆 | Runner beans 紅花菜豆 |

| Chayote 佛手瓜 | Autumn cup squash 日本南瓜 | Butternut squash 奶油南瓜 | Sweet Dumpling squash 迷你甜南瓜 | Pumpkin 南瓜 | Spaghetti squash 金絲南瓜 |

| Button mushrooms 草菇 | Porcini mushrooms 牛肝菌菇 | Shiitake mushrooms 香菇 | Portobello mushroom 大啡菇 | Oyster mushrooms 杏鮑菇 | Enoki mushrooms 金針菇 |

Purple haze
carrots
紫蘿蔔

Carrot
胡蘿蔔

Taro
芋頭

Celeriac
塊根芹

Turnip
蕪菁

Maca
瑪卡

Leek
韭葱

Brown onion
洋葱

White onion
白洋葱

Shallots
紅葱頭

Garlic
大蒜

Spring onions
葱

Pearl onions
珍珠洋葱

Red onion
紫洋葱

Anya potato
安雅馬鈴薯

Maris Piper potato
梅莉斯笛手馬鈴薯

Charlotte potato
夏洛特馬鈴薯

Jersey
Royal new
potatoes
澤西皇家新薯

Désirée potato
澳洲玫瑰紅薯

Russet potato
褐皮馬鈴薯

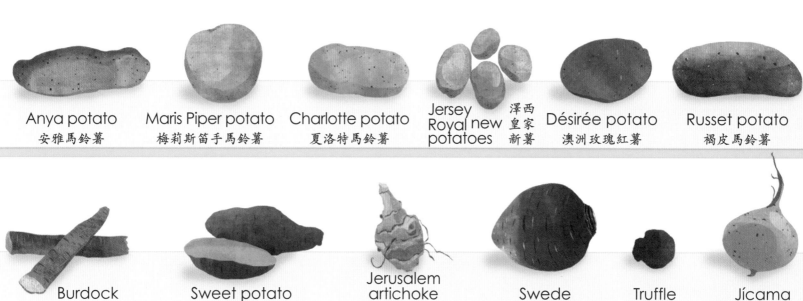

Burdock
牛蒡

Sweet potato
蕃薯

Jerusalem
artichoke
菊芋

Swede
瑞典蕪菁

Truffle
松露

Jícama
沙葛

Parsnip
歐防風

Salsify
婆羅門參

Yacón
雪蓮薯

Lotus root
蓮藕

Water chestnut
荸薺

Cassava
木薯

Beetroot
紅菜頭

Radish
小紅蘿蔔

Fennel
茴香

Daikon
白蘿蔔

Yam
山藥

Kohlrabi
大頭菜

Purple sprouting broccoli
紫球花椰菜

Broccoli
西蘭花

Brussels sprouts
抱子甘藍

Spring greens
嫩洋白菜葉

Swiss chard
瑞士甜菜

Spinach
菠菜

Savoy cabbage
皺葉椰菜

Kale
羽衣甘藍

Chinese broccoli
芥蘭

Collard greens
芥蘭菜葉

Black kale
黑葉甘藍

Pak choi
白菜

Avocado
牛油果

Cress
水芹

Frisée lettuce
九芽菜

Rocket
火箭菜

Iceberg lettuce
卷心生菜

Cucumber
青瓜

Cos lettuce
羅馬生菜

Radiccio
紅菊苣

Watercress
西洋菜

Tomatillos
墨西哥綠番茄

Cherry tomatoes
車厘茄

Pear tomato
梨茄

Beef tomato
牛茄

Plum tomato
羅馬番茄

Herbs 香草

Tarragon
龍蒿

Rosemary
迷迭香

Sage
鼠尾草

Lemongrass
檸檬香茅

Dill
蒔蘿

Basil
羅勒

Oregano
牛至

Coriander
芫荽

Flat leaf parsley
平葉歐芹

Curly leaf parsley
捲葉歐芹

Chives
細青蔥

Thyme
百里香

Lemon thyme
檸檬百里香

Mint
薄荷

Marjoram
馬鬱蘭

Bay leaves
月桂葉

16

The fishmonger 魚販

Cod 鱈魚

Hake 無鬚鱈魚

Tuna 吞拿魚   Salmon 三文魚   Pollock 青鱈   Red mullet 紅鯔魚   Grey mullet 烏頭

Red snapper 紅鯛魚   Sea bass 海鱸魚   Trout 鱒魚   Haddock 黑線鱈魚   Mackerel 鯖魚

Lemon sole 檸鰈魚   Dover sole 龍脷魚   Plaice 鰈魚   Turbot 比目魚   Brill 鰈魚

Sea bream 鯛魚   Carp 鯉魚   Catfish 鯰魚   Swordfish 劍魚   Monkfish 鮟鱇魚

Herring 鯡魚   Whitebait 銀魚   Anchovies 鯷魚   Squid 魷魚   Sardine 沙甸魚

Lobster 龍蝦   Crab 蟹   Prawns 蝦   Langoustine 海螯蝦   Octopus 章魚

Crayfish 螯蝦   Mussels 青口   Clams 蛤   Razor clams 竹蟶   Cockles 蛤蜊   Scallop 扇貝

Oysters 蠔   Salmon roe 三文魚籽   Beluga caviar 魚子醬   Jellied eels 鱔魚凍   Rollmop herrings 醋漬鯡魚捲   Kippers 醃鯡魚

The butcher 肉販

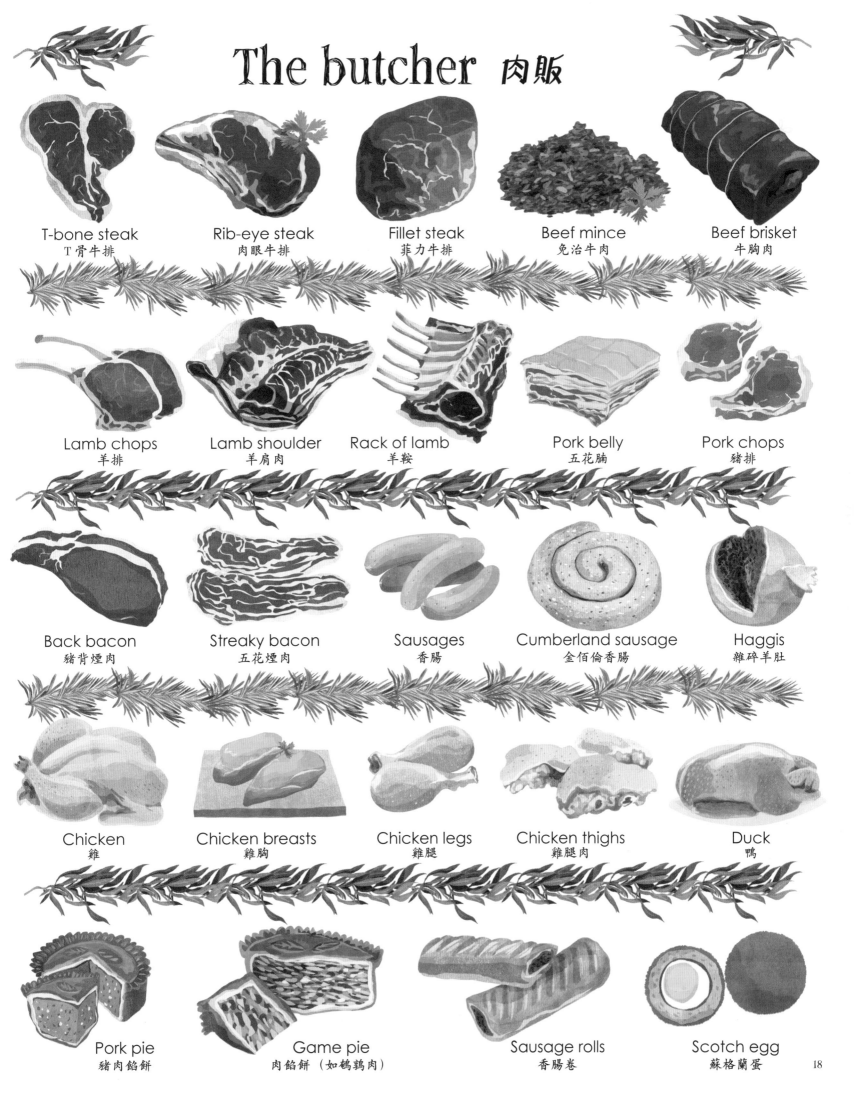

T-bone steak
T骨牛排

Rib-eye steak
肉眼牛排

Fillet steak
菲力牛排

Beef mince
免治牛肉

Beef brisket
牛胸肉

Lamb chops
羊排

Lamb shoulder
羊肩肉

Rack of lamb
羊鞍

Pork belly
五花腩

Pork chops
豬排

Back bacon
豬背煙肉

Streaky bacon
五花煙肉

Sausages
香腸

Cumberland sausage
金佰倫香腸

Haggis
雜碎羊肚

Chicken
雞

Chicken breasts
雞胸

Chicken legs
雞腿

Chicken thighs
雞腿肉

Duck
鴨

Pork pie
豬肉餡餅

Game pie
肉餡餅（如鵪鶉肉）

Sausage rolls
香腸卷

Scotch egg
蘇格蘭蛋

The deli 熟食店

Cream cheese
忌廉芝士

Gorgonzola
哥根蘇拿芝士

Pecorino
羅馬羊奶芝士

Cottage cheese
茅屋芝士

Red Leicester
紅萊斯特芝士

Feta
菲達芝士

Manchego
曼徹格芝士

Ricotta
鄉村芝士

Fontina
芳提娜芝士

Emmental
埃文達芝士

Parmesan
巴馬臣芝士

Cheddar
車打芝士

Mozzarella
水牛芝士

Stilton
斯蒂爾頓芝士

Brie
布利芝士

Camembert
金銀幣芝士

Le roulé
芝士卷

Roquefort
羅克福藍芝士

Monterey Jack
蒙特里積芝士

Goat's cheese
山羊芝士

Havarti
哈瓦蒂芝士

Sheep's cheese
綿羊芝士

Gruyère
格魯耶亞芝士

Edam
艾登芝士

Chorizo
西班牙辣肉腸

Prosciutto
意大利火腿

Parma ham
巴馬火腿

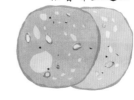
Mortadella
意式肉腸

Beef carpaccio
生牛肉薄片

Pancetta
意大利醃肉

Bresaola
意大利風乾牛肉

Pepperoni
意大利辣肉腸

Bratwurst
油煎香腸

Polish sausage
波蘭香腸

Ham slice
火腿切片

Serrano ham
西班牙火腿

Pastrami
燻牛肉

Salami
莎樂美腸

Stuffed peppadew
peppers 釀甜椒

Brussels pâté
布魯塞爾肉醬

Duck and orange
pâté
香橙鴨肉醬

Ardennes pâté
阿登肉批

Green olives
綠橄欖

Black olives
黑橄欖

Sundried
tomatoes
番茄乾

The sweet shop 糖果店

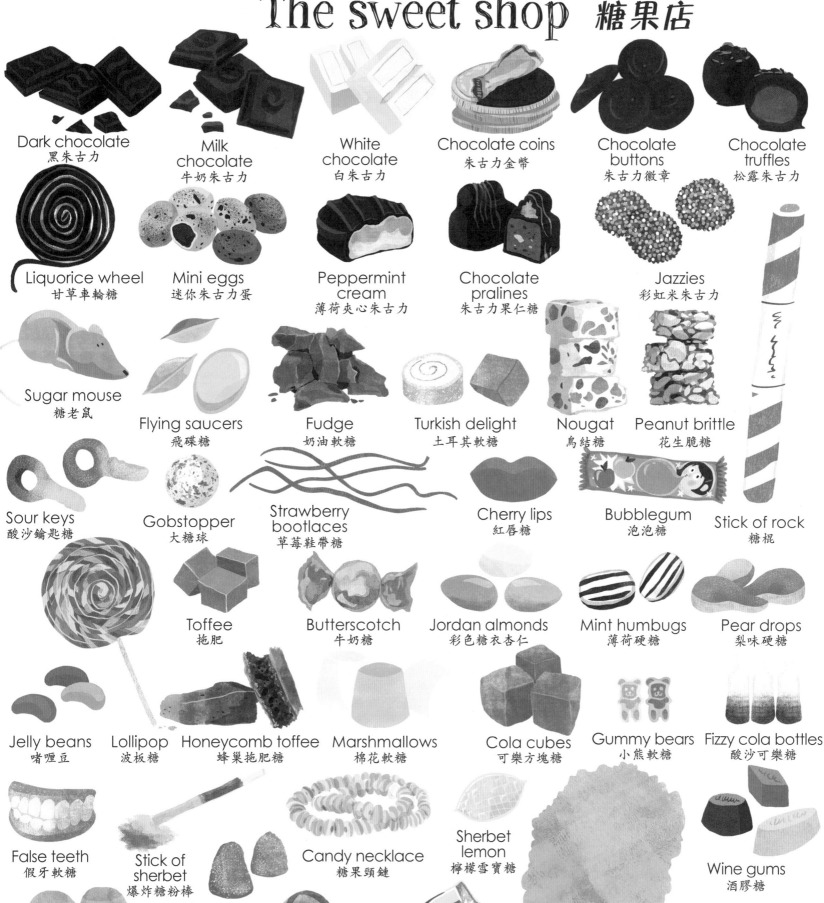

Dark chocolate 黑朱古力

Milk chocolate 牛奶朱古力

White chocolate 白朱古力

Chocolate coins 朱古力金幣

Chocolate buttons 朱古力徽章

Chocolate truffles 松露朱古力

Liquorice wheel 甘草車輪糖

Mini eggs 迷你朱古力蛋

Peppermint cream 薄荷夾心朱古力

Chocolate pralines 朱古力果仁糖

Jazzies 彩虹米朱古力

Sugar mouse 糖老鼠

Flying saucers 飛碟糖

Fudge 奶油軟糖

Turkish delight 土耳其軟糖

Nougat 鳥結糖

Peanut brittle 花生脆糖

Sour keys 酸沙鑰匙糖

Gobstopper 大糖球

Strawberry bootlaces 草莓鞋帶糖

Cherry lips 紅唇糖

Bubblegum 泡泡糖

Stick of rock 糖棍

Toffee 拖肥

Butterscotch 牛奶糖

Jordan almonds 彩色糖衣杏仁

Mint humbugs 薄荷硬糖

Pear drops 梨味硬糖

Jelly beans 啫喱豆

Lollipop 波板糖

Honeycomb toffee 蜂巢拖肥糖

Marshmallows 棉花軟糖

Cola cubes 可樂方塊糖

Gummy bears 小熊軟糖

Fizzy cola bottles 酸沙可樂糖

False teeth 假牙軟糖

Stick of sherbet 爆炸糖粉棒

Candy necklace 糖果頸鏈

Sherbet lemon 檸檬雪寶糖

Wine gums 酒膠糖

Strawberry bonbons 草莓糖

Gumdrops 橡皮糖

Rainbow belt 彩虹腰帶糖

Popping candy 爆炸糖

Candy floss 棉花糖

Fried egg sweets 蛋糖

Coffee shop 咖啡店

Granola bar
燕麥營養棒

Almond croissant
杏仁牛角酥

Chocolate twist
朱古力扭紋包

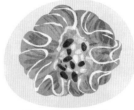
Danish pastry
丹麥麵包

Pain aux raisins
葡萄乾丹麥卷

Lemon cake
檸檬蛋糕

Millionaire's shortbread
百萬富翁酥餅

Blueberry muffin
藍莓鬆餅

Chocolate muffin
朱古力鬆餅

Teacakes
茶點圓餅

Panini
帕尼尼三文治

Ham and cheese toastie
火腿芝士飛碟

Hot chocolate
熱朱古力

Coffee
咖啡

Green tea
綠茶

Fish restaurant 海鮮餐廳

Smoked salmon
煙三文魚

Gravlax
醃製三文魚

Bisque
海鮮濃湯

Salt cod
鹽醃鱈魚

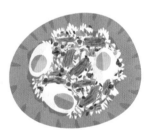
Kedgeree
雞蛋葱豆燴飯

Calamari
魷魚圈

Fish cakes
炸魚餅

Crab cakes
蟹肉餅

Lobster
龍蝦

Tuna steak
吞拿魚排

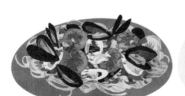
Fruits de mer
linguine
海鮮扁意粉

Bouillabaisse
馬賽魚湯

Fish soup
海鮮湯

Moules
marinières
白酒煮青口

Fish goujons
麵包糠炸魚柳

21

Out for lunch 外出午膳

Tuna melt
吞拿魚芝士三文治

Cheese on toast
芝士吐司

Steak and kidney pie
牛排腰子餡餅

Smoothie
沙冰

Fizzy water
氣泡水

Milkshake
奶昔

BLT
煙肉生菜番茄三文治

Club sandwich
公司三文治

Prawn mayonnaise sandwich
大蝦沙律三文治

Fish fingers
炸魚柳條

Fish and chips
炸魚薯條

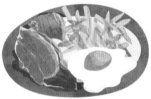    

Gammon, egg and chips
醃豬腿煎蛋薯條

Onion rings
洋蔥圈

Scampi and fries
炸大蝦配薯條

Chicken and mushroom pie
雞肉蘑菇餡餅

Stuffed peppers
釀甜椒炒飯

Cheese and onion pasty
芝士洋蔥餡餅

Omelette
奄列

Quiche Lorraine
法式洛林餡餅

French onion soup
法式洋蔥湯

Ham hock
德國鹹豬手

Potato salad
馬鈴薯沙律

Beefburger
牛肉漢堡

Cheeseburger
芝士漢堡

Chicken nuggets
炸雞塊

Lamb hotpot
馬鈴薯燉羊肉

Niçoise salad
尼斯沙律

Green salad
生菜沙律

Caesar salad
凱撒沙律

Russian salad
俄羅斯沙律

Coleslaw
椰菜沙律

Italian restaurant
意大利餐廳

Bruschetta
普切塔番茄香料麵包

Grissini
麵包脆棒

Garlic bread
蒜蓉包

Melanzane parmigiana
焗烤千層茄子

Insalata caprese
卡布里沙律

Risotto
意大利燴飯

Lasagne
意大利千層麵

Rotolo
麵卷

Calzone pizza
口袋薄餅

Arancini
炸飯糰

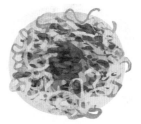

Tagliatelle al ragu
肉醬寬扁麵

Ravioli
意大利餃

Gnocchi
馬鈴薯丸子

Pasta and pesto
青醬意粉

Spaghetti alla
carbonara
卡邦尼意粉

Quattro stagioni pizza
四季薄餅

Margherita pizza
瑪格麗塔薄餅

Bucatini all'amatriciana
辣煙肉番茄吸管麵

Penne all'arrabbiata
香辣茄醬直通粉

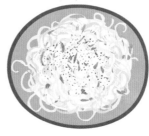

Fettuccine alfredo
白醬緞帶麵

Spaghetti alle vongole
白酒蜆肉意粉

Tortelloni
意大利雲吞

Tortellini
意大利方雲吞

Tiramisu
提拉米蘇

Zabaglione
沙巴翁

Spanish restaurant
西班牙餐廳

Ajoblanco
大蒜杏仁冷湯

Spanish tortilla
馬鈴薯蛋餅

Patatas bravas
香辣炸馬鈴薯

Gazpacho
西班牙番茄冷湯

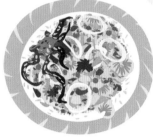

Paella
西班牙海鮮燉飯

Turrón
杜隆杏仁糖

Mexican and Southern American restaurant
墨西哥南美餐廳

Burrito
墨西哥捲餅

Enchilada
墨西哥春卷

Quesadilla
墨西哥芝士餡餅

Tacos
墨西哥玉米捲餅

Tamales
墨西哥粽

Pico de gallo
公雞嘴醬

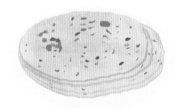

Tortillas
墨西哥薄餅

Arroz con pollo
雞肉焗飯

Guacamole
牛油果莎莎醬

Chile verde
綠辣椒燉豬肉

Ceviche
檸汁醃魚生

Gumbo
秋葵濃湯

Refried beans
豆蓉

Fried chicken
炸雞

Shrimp and grits
鮮蝦玉米粥

Jambalaya
雜錦飯

Tres leches
三奶蛋糕

Mississippi mud pie
密西西比軟泥餡餅

Bombay mix
香豆花生雜錦

Indian restaurant
印度餐廳

Mango chutney
芒果酸甜醬

Lime pickle
印度醃漬青檸

Poppadoms
印度薄餅

Raita
青瓜乳酪

Dosa
多薩米餅

Onion bhajis
炸洋蔥絲

Vegetable pakoras
炸雜菜

Samosas
咖哩角

Saag paneer
菠菜蓉燴芝士

Prawn bhuna
香汁蝦

Biryani
印度香飯

Dal
燉扁豆

Chicken tikka
印度燒雞塊

Chana masala
鷹嘴豆咖哩

Vindaloo
酸咖喱肉

Tandoori chicken
天多利燒雞

Chicken korma
奶油燉雞

Aloo gobhi
咖哩馬鈴薯椰菜花

Chapati
全麥薄餅

Naan
印度烤餅

Roti
印度薄餅

Pilau rice
香料飯

Lassi
印度酸乳酪

Kulfi
印度牛奶冰

25

Prawn
crackers
蝦片

Fortune
cookie
幸運餅乾

Chinese restaurant
中式餐廳

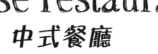

Spring rolls
春卷

Dumplings
餃子

Prawn toast
蝦多士

Fried rice
炒飯

Rice noodles
米粉

Crispy seaweed
炸紫菜

Chow mein
炒麵

Kung Pao
chicken
宮保雞丁

Peking duck
北京填鴨

Spare ribs
排骨

Wonton soup
雲吞湯麵

Sweet and
sour chicken
咕嚕雞球

Shredded chilli
beef
辣椒牛肉絲

Char siu pork
叉燒

Chop suey
炒雜碎

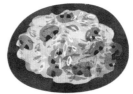
Egg foo yung
芙蓉蛋

Mapo tofu
麻婆豆腐

Mooncakes
月餅

Japanese restaurant 日式餐廳

Tuna sashimi
吞拿魚刺身

Maki
卷壽司

Futomaki
太卷

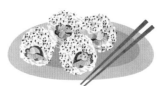
Uramaki
反卷

Salmon nigiri
三文魚壽司

Prawn
tempura
炸蝦天婦羅

Chicken teriyaki
照燒雞肉

Gyoza
煎餃子

Katsu curry
咖喱炸豬排

Temaki
手卷

Yakitore
烤雞肉串

Udon
烏冬

Ramen
拉麵

Pickled ginger
酸薑

Wasabi sauce
芥末醬

Miso soup
味噌湯

Flatbread
烤包

Middle Eastern restaurant
中東餐廳

Pitta bread
比得包

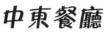

Koftas
免治肉串

Shakshuka
北非蛋

Pilaf
手抓飯

Shish kebab
烤羊肉串

Lamb tagine
塔吉鍋炖羊

Tabbouleh
塔布勒沙律

Tahdig
鍋巴米飯

Kibbeh
黎巴嫩肉丸

Fattoush
阿拉伯蔬菜沙律

Merguez
北非辣肉腸

Hummus
鷹嘴豆蓉

Falafel
鷹嘴豆餅

Sujuk
辣碎肉腸

Ful medames
蠶豆湯

Pastilla
雞肉果仁千層批

Doner kebab
土耳其卡巴

Baba ghanoush
茄泥沾醬

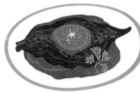

Karnıyarık
茄鑲肉末

Halva
哈爾瓦酥糖

Mint tea
薄荷茶

Baklava
果仁蜜餅

Kanafeh
庫納法

Greek restaurant 希臘餐廳

Tzatziki
青瓜酸乳酪醬汁

Moussaka
慕薩卡肉醬千層餡餅

Beef stifado
希臘式紅酒燉牛肉

Greek salad
希臘沙拉

Taramasalata
紅魚子泥沙律

Fried halloumi
炸哈羅米芝士

Dolmades
酸葡萄葉釀飯

Souvlakia
串燒捲餅

Kleftiko
土匪羊

Spanakopita
菠菜批

Galaktoboureko
千層牛奶玉米糕

Greek yogurt
希臘乳酪

Southeast Asian restaurant
東南亞餐廳

Gado-gado
印尼加多加多沙律

Nasi goreng
印尼炒飯

Som tam
青木瓜沙律

Pho
越南河粉

Chicken satay
沙嗲雞串

Tom yum
冬蔭功

Thai green curry
泰式青咖喱

Thai red curry
泰式紅咖喱

Pad Thai
泰式炒金邊粉

Street food
街頭小吃

Bánh mì
越南法包

Hot dog
熱狗

Churros
吉拿棒

Nachos
墨西哥玉米片

Bunny chow
咖喱吐司盒

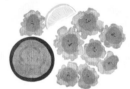
Fried plantain
炸大蕉

Pão de queijo
芝士麵包球

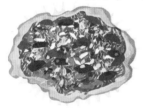
Papri chaat
乳酪伴威化

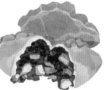
Empanada
恩潘納達烤餃子

Cornish pasty
康沃爾肉餡餅

Gatsby sandwich
南非三文治

Pretzels
椒鹽卷餅

Chicken wings
雞翼

Pulled pork sandwich
手撕豬肉三文治

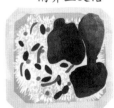
Jerk chicken with rice and peas
牙買加烤雞飯

Shawarma
沙威瑪旋轉烤肉卷

Pav bhaji
蔬菜咖喱配餐包

Crêpe
法國薄餅

Currywurst
德國咖喱腸

Pani puri
印度炸脆餅

Festivals and celebrations 節慶

Birthday party 生日派對

Chocolate cake
朱古力蛋糕

Cocktail sausages
雞尾腸

Cherryade
櫻桃汽水

Cola
可樂

Orange squash
鮮橙雜飲

Lemonade
檸檬汁

Ginger beer
薑啤

Popcorn
爆谷

Crisps
薯片

Chicken drumsticks
雞腿

Cheese twists
芝士條

Ramadan and Eid-ul-Fitr 齋戒月及開齋節

Dates
椰棗

Ma'amoul
椰棗餅

Qatayef
黃金甜餃

Jalebi
炸線圈

Haleem
谷物燉肉粥

Gulab jamun
玫瑰果

Dahi baray
乳酪泡餅

Luqaimat
炸糖丸

Sheer Khurma
椰棗乾布甸

Lachha paratha
拉卡油餅

Chinese New Year 農曆新年

Buddha's delight
佛跳牆

Jau gok
角仔

Mandarin oranges
年桔

Nian gao
年糕

Kueh bangkit
番婆餅

Diwali 排燈節   ## Gurpurbs 錫克教

Barfi
牛奶糕

Laddu
小甜球

Shakkar para
甜方脆

Balushahi
印度糖脆冬甩

Karah Parshad
酥糖

Christmas 聖誕節

Cranberry sauce
蔓越莓醬

Stuffing
火雞餡料

Pigs in blankets
熱狗捲

Baked ham
烤火腿

Roast goose
烤鵝

Roast turkey
烤火雞

Gravy
肉汁醬

Candy cane
士的糖

Fruit cake
水果蛋糕

Gingerbread house
薑餅人屋

Yule log
聖誕樹頭蛋糕

Panettone
托尼甜麵包

Stollen
史多倫麵包

Lebkuchen
德國薑餅

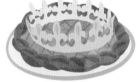
Galette des rois
國王餅

Kringle
糖霜餅乾

Mince pie
甜餡餅

Christmas pudding
聖誕布甸

Thanksgiving 感恩節

Pecan pie
山核桃餡餅

Pumpkin pie
南瓜餡餅

Sweet potato casserole
焗蕃薯蓉

Dumplings
紅薯餃子

Easter 復活節

Simnel cake
杏仁水果蛋糕

Easter egg
復活蛋

Hot cross bun
十字麵包

Chocolate rabbit
兔子朱古力

Tsoureki
希臘甜麵包

Passover 逾越節

Matzo balls
猶太湯丸

Charoset
甜泥醬

Gefilte fish
燉魚丸

Matzo
無酵餅

Rosh Hashanah 猶太新年　　Hannukkah 光明節　　Purim 普珥節

Tzimmes
燉蔬菜乾果

Sufganiyah
猶太果醬冬甩

Latke
馬鈴薯餅

Hamantashen
三角餅乾

Desserts and cakes 甜品和蛋糕

Ice cream cone
甜筒

Panna cotta
意式奶凍

Fruit salad
水果沙律

Crème brûlée
法式焦糖燉蛋

Poached pear
紅酒燉梨

Ice cream sundae
雪糕新地

Crème caramel
焦糖布甸

Profiteroles
泡芙

Îles flottantes
漂浮之島

Banana split
香蕉船

Lemon meringue pie
檸檬蛋白餡餅

Trifle
乳脂鬆糕

Summer pudding
夏令布甸

Belgian waffles
比利時窩夫

Treacle tart
糖漿餡餅

Jam doughnut
炸果醬麵包

Sugar doughnut
砂糖冬甩

Iced doughnut
糖霜冬甩

Tarte tatin
反烤蘋果撻

Dulce de leche
牛奶焦糖醬

Granita
意大利沙冰

Sorbet
雪葩

Jelly
啫喱

Pavlova
百露華蛋糕

Baked Alaska
焗火焰雪山

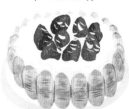
Angel food cake
天使蛋糕

Key lime pie
美式檸檬餡餅

Clafoutis
法式櫻桃撻

Bakewell tart
杏仁撻

Black forest gâteau
黑森林蛋糕

Rice pudding
米布甸

Chocolate fondant
熔岩朱古力蛋糕

Chocolate mousse
朱古力慕絲蛋糕

Chocolate bombe
朱古力雪糕蛋糕

Whipping cream
鮮忌廉

Pouring cream
忌廉

1000 Things to Eat
Copyright © 2015, 2018 Usborne Publishing Limited.
Chinese Mandarin (using complex characters) Translation
Copyright © 2019 The Commercial Press (H.K.) Ltd.

書名：兒童英漢詞彙大書 —— 食物 1000 詞
作者：Hannah Wood
繪圖：Nikki Dyson
出版：商務印書館 (香港) 有限公司
　　　香港筲箕灣耀興道 3 號東滙廣場 8 樓
　　　http://www.commercialpress.com.hk
發行：香港聯合書刊物流有限公司
　　　香港新界荃灣德士古道 220-248 號荃灣工業中心 16 樓
版次：2024 年 7 月第 1 版第 2 次印刷
　　　©2019 商務印書館 (香港) 有限公司
　　　ISBN 978 962 07 0566 3
　　　版權所有　不得翻印